¡Gazpacho!

LORENZO ELIANO

Heads or Tales Press

ISBN: 978-1-912704-30-9

DEDICATION

For

Linda who dreamt of going to Thailand but
never did.

Table of Contents

ACKNOWLEDGMENTS

Cover designed by Jennifer Cabatuan

1

Heathrow Airport, London

Nicholas Briddick tapped at his MacBook. Weirdly, the British Airways first class departure lounge always inspired him. Maybe it was the mahogany tables, black leather sofas and the extra long bar. Especially the bar. He'd never completed a film script without keeping his alcohol levels high. He was a cross between Rob Reiner in looks, and Ridley Scott in movie direction. His greying beard was prickly and his attitude matched his beard. As he typed, his mobile phone rang with the theme tune to one of his own movies. He groaned when he saw the name on the screen. Why couldn't she leave him alone?

"Hi darling," Nicholas breathed heavily when speaking. He drank, he smoked cigars, he liked subs. "No, of course not. It's not for long. I'll be back before you can clip all of Sylvester's nails." He carried on typing. "You know I do. You know... I love you." Nicholas hung up his mobile phone, shook his head and groaned again then resumed typing.

Ricki Singh, precision-cut facial hair, sunglasses that he wore day or night, indoors and out, a muscle T-shirt to show off his muscular physique, swaggered over to Nicholas with the air of a Bollywood superstar – which he was.

"Nicholas Briddick?" Ricki kept on his sunglasses.

Nicholas glanced up for the briefest of moments then resumed his work.

"Mr Briddick. Sir, may I sit down?" Ricki confidently sat himself alongside Nicholas, who hadn't even paused, besides sipping from a glass of his Beringer Private Reserve Chardonnay. Ricki held up his hand to the barman, "Give me what he's having. And another for my friend, Mr Briddick? No?"

Ricki was a persistent cat. He hadn't risen to the top standing idly by. "I'm a big fan of your movies, Nicholas. May I call you Nicholas? You're one of my favourite directors.

Nicholas was equally as persistent in ignoring him.

"I've been told I have a substantial following. Hell, I know I have!" Ricki held out a hand expecting it to be shaken – which it wasn't. "My name is Ricki Singh, perhaps you've heard of me?"

"Sorry." Nicholas continued his resistance.

Ricki got his wine and had a taste. "Primo wine! You have Wi-Fi here?"

"It's 2016. We're in the first class departure lounge at Heathrow. I'd bloody expect so," Nicholas said curtly.

"Great, yaar because then you can Google me and see for yourself that I am one of Bollywood's most bankable stars."

"Look, I'm a little busy."

"Writing your new movie?"

"Maybe."

"My agent's really got his finger on the pulse and he told me you're making a new blockbuster. I'd be great in it."

"Is that so?"

"Absolutely. I've already cracked the Asian market. Now it's time for a new challenge. To conquer America."

Nicholas sighed a sigh that caused a miniature

tornado to sweep through Hounslow. He closed his laptop shut and gave his full attention to Ricki, not before rolling his eyes.

"I'm the biggest star in India. Women want me, guys wanna be me and children idolise me."

"You have a high opinion of yourself."

"When you receive as much adoration as I do, it happens, yaar."

"No one knows you in America. I don't know you."

"For now. I'm sure your movie will do well in India, but think about this: with me in it, it will do a thousand times better!"

"We're still a long way from casting, so I can't really promise anything."

"I appreciate that. Here, let me give you my card." Ricki produced a flashy business card that would've been the envy of Patrick Bateman. Nicholas took the card without a word.

"You know, I was gutted when *The Tin House* didn't win the Oscar. It was a travesty."

"The politics of Hollywood. It affects the best of us."

"But why to you always? What is it now, five nominations and no wins? I mean it's a disgrace."

"Right." Nicholas took a swig of his wine. His throat had gotten dry and there was a pain in his ears.

"Exactly. I mean, a director of your ability. It's completely illogical."

"Maybe next time."

"I hope so. If not, then I will go to Hollywood and bash their heads together."

"I'm sure that won't be necessary."

"Probably. You've been in the industry for so

long, you're bound to pick up an Honorary Oscar at the very least!"

"Listen, I must get back to my work." Nicholas reopened his laptop. He was going to hire personal security in future.

"Sure, I understand. Where are you flying to?"

"New York."

"Cool. The Big Apple. I've been many times; it's like my second home. I'm thinking of buying an apartment out there. Do you live in New York?"

"No. I live in London."

"Cool. I like London too. I have many good friends here."

An awkward silence descended that would've disturbed even David Blaine. Ricki took out a Toblerone and hungrily devoured it like he was Hannibal and it was human flesh. It wasn't the huge Toblerone. Ricki left a piece.

"Would you like some?" Ricki offered.

"No, I'm fine."

"I was in London promoting my latest movie. *Nightmares in Paradise*'. Catchy title, yaar?"

"Very."

"Yeah, it stars me and this real hot cutie, Sonal Prakash. If you saw her, man, you wouldn't be able to walk normally for a week!"

"I'm happily married."

"Marriage is good. But if I got married, 400 million women would simultaneously commit suicide."

"You must be quite busy."

"You're telling me. I barely have enough time to eat or sleep. I bet you know all about that, yaar?"

"Excuse me?"

"You were around in the sixties, all that free

love and female liberation."

"I'm 58."

"Ah, now the seventies, that was a time to party. I bet you were a busy bee in your heyday."

"Not really."

"Look at my Gene Simmons impression." Ricki stuck his tongue out and waggled it. "He slept with 4,000 women. Did you know that?"

"4,800."

"Not as much as you, eh?" Ricki nudged Nicholas with his arm, winked then laughed causing lattes not to be sipped temporarily. "Sure you did, sure you did. You know, every morning I wake up and I expect to find another woman outside my door with a babe in arms."

"Maybe you should be more careful."

"Yeah, you're right. But I want to have fun while I'm young and when you have gorgeous naked women throwing themselves at you, what can you do?"

"Show a little restraint?"

"You're a funny guy. I remember that one movie you made, I was laughing so hard I nearly shit my pants. What was it called?"

"*Fifth Street*?"

"No. Oh, now I remember. *Chronicles of a Mad Man*."

"That wasn't a comedy."

"No? But it was so funny, I had popcorn coming out of my arse."

"Anyway, this script won't write itself..."

"Listen Nicholas, man, I have to come clean."

"About what? I'm not the police."

"Well, like I said, my agent really has his fingers on the pulse. So I knew you'd be here."

Nicholas raised his eyebrows higher than London property prices. "Why? Is he keeping tabs on me?"

"Your new movie. I need to be in it."

"Like I said..."

"I know but we're both men of the world, yaar? Maybe we could come to a deal?"

"What kind of deal?"

"I'm from a rich family, Nicholas. Name a price that gets me a role in this movie."

"You're that desperate?"

"I deserve to be a global star. I want everyone in America to know the name Ricki Singh."

"Ricki, this isn't how I cast my films. I don't sell roles."

"Don't think of it as selling a role, think of it as doing a good turn."

"How would I be doing a good turn?"

"Tell me something, how many superstars in Hollywood are Asian?"

"There's Jackie Chan."

"But how many are from the Indian subcontinent? None! And yet more than one sixth of the world's population is from there."

"So?"

"Hollywood's racist. Maybe not against black people or those kung fu kicking bastards from the Far East but against us."

"I don't select actors by race, I choose the one that is best for the role."

"And I am the best. The world is crying out for an Indian Hollywood star. Think of all those ABI's and BBI's who have no idol to worship."

"AB... What?"

"American and British born Indians. So, how about it? We got a deal?"

"Look Ricki, I understand where you're coming from but this isn't how I operate. You're more than welcome to audition that's the best I can do."

Ricki bowed his head. He looked like a lost puppy that had been abandoned for the second Christmas in a row.

A robotic voice echoed from the tannoy, "British Airways flight BA 117 to New York J.F.K. now boarding at Gate B34."

"That's me." Nicholas hurriedly packed up his stuff. Thank fuck for that!

"Wait, Nicholas, sir. Let me show you my Marlon Brando in *The Godfather*." Ricki coughed, slicked his hair back then, in Al Pacino's *Scarface* voice, recited, "'In this country, you gotta make the money first. Then when you get the money, you get the power. Then when you get the power, then you get the women.' Eh? What do you think?"

Nicholas started to turn away from Ricki.

"Wait! Watch this." Ricki, to the dismay of Nicholas and every other sane person in the departure lounge, then performed the chorus of 'Jai Ho' complete with a short dance and an unexpected backflip - unexpected for him too as he landed awkwardly slap on his back. "Sisterfucker! My back!"

"I'll be in touch." Nicholas departed quicker than even he knew his stubby legs could carry him. Ricki remained lying down.

"Cool. I'll be waiting!" Ricki, favouring his back, gingerly got up. Out of the corner of his eye he spotted Anna Banks, a slender brunette with an angelic face carrying an LV handbag. She was often compared to Anne Hathaway for both her looks and acting ability.

"Anna!" Ricki shouted, disturbing everybody yet again. He grimaced and held his lower back, then headed over to where Anna was seated. "Anna Banks! My god! It's so great to meet you."

Anna glanced about her. The feeling wasn't mutual. "Likewise."

"Great. My name's Ricki Singh, maybe you've heard of me? You know, you and I would be great in that movie I hear you're making."

2

Dubai International Airport

Tony Wong, a Taiwanese with a ponytail and 1970s movie moustache was sitting outside a duty-free shop. He had obviously eaten too much dim sum in his life as his white shirt took on an unnatural shape and his black leather coat had given up the struggle to ever be buttoned again. He flicked through a newspaper that he didn't bother to read.

Ricki, wearing a baseball cap and those ever-present sunglasses, emerged carrying a cup of overpriced coffee with a ton of shit on top that detracted from the coffee. He also had a Bollywood movie magazine with him. He parked himself near Tony who moved over towards Ricki discreetly.

"Mr Singh." Tony had a cold as ice voice.

"Mr Chang? I'm happy you could meet me," Ricki whispered.

"You want another coffee?"

"No thanks. This is already my third."

"Where you flying today?"

"Back to Mumbai. You?"

"I'm told you have a problem."

"Yes, yes I do. I hear that you help people." Ricki ran his hand through his hair. He wasn't sure if his hand then appeared wet because of the product in his hair or because of his nerves.

"Like an exclusive Samaritan. What can I do for you?"

Ricki slid over a studio publicity photo of another Bollywood matinee idol. An actor with jet black hair, just styled, and with a Derek Zoolander 'Blue

Steel' face.

"Ravi Puri?"

"You know him?"

"I'm a big Bollywood fan. I know you too."

"Of course. You like my films?"

"Why's he a problem?"

"He's competition. He's the next big thing, the one everyone wants to see. His shitty face is on the cover of all the magazines and he has more Facebook fan pages than me. He even has more likes and more Instagram followers!"

"Competition never hurt."

"It's hurting me. I'm number one but with this mama's boy around, I might not be."

"What do you want done?"

"I want my headache to go away."

"My medicine is expensive."

"Money is not an issue."

Tony took out an orange Bic pen and wrote a figure on his newspaper.

"This is my rate, plus expenses. I need half the sum to be wired now and the rest when on completion. Agreed, Mr Singh?"

"Please, call me Ricki."

"Mr Singh, I have many people asking for my help. Sometimes I don't take the job because the client is nervous."

"I can pay more if that will help you relax."

"How do you know Ravi Puri won't just be another shooting star?"

"The studios are really behind him. There's too much money on Ravi for him to be a flash in the pan."

"But there must be room in Bollywood for the two of you?"

"If he keeps going, I'll be yesterday's news. Nothing beats being number one, just as nothing's worse than being washed up."

"I can cure one headache, but there'll be another around the corner."

"I'll deal with it then. Right now I'm still consolidating my position, so I'm vulnerable."

"No offence, Mr Singh, but I don't buy it. You're employing me because Ravi Puri's going to be a bigger star? If we're going to do business then let's cut the bullshit."

"He thinks I slept with his younger sister."

"Did you?"

"Yaar, she's a real hottie. Twenty, with tits like this…" Ricki held his hands out to about a fraction less than double Ds.

"So why do you need me to blackmail him?"

"This sisterfucker accused me of raping her. It could ruin me."

"Why's he think that?"

"Because he's pissed off. I tell you, these people chose the wrong family to fuck with."

Tony received a message text message. The ring tune was the Katy Perry song, *Roar*.

"Good tune." Ricki bobbed his head.

Tony checked the message out of view from Ricki.

"I need you to make half the transfer now. When my account has received the funds, I'll know you're serious."

"I can do that."

Tony slid across a card. "This isn't very professional but I have daughter and she's a big fan. Could you sign something for her?"

"Your daughter?"

"Yeah, she's crazy about you."

"What do you want me to sign?"

"I have a photo of you, for ID, you understand?"

Tony whipped the folded photo out of a Manila envelope from inside his jacket pocket.

"Whom should I make it out to?"

"Make it out to... Sorry, I lied. It's for me."

"To Mr Chang?"

"No. If you just sign and date, it's fine."

"There you go."

"Thank you."

Tony picked up his treasured autographed photo and left. Ricki strolled over to a duty-free shop, taking his Bollywood movie magazine with him. The kind of bright, white duty-free shop that showed up your flaws and blemishes, it was filled with fragrances, alcohol and other still over-priced goods. Ricki browsed through the colognes, testing and sniffing them like a true connoisseur.

A petite Filipina perfumery assistant in a whiter than white, white uniform, approached. "Can I be of assistance, sir?"

"You could assist me by telling me what chat up line would work best on you?"

Sylvia blushed, which was hard to see through the amount of makeup she was forced to wear. Though it was also handy to have so much makeup on - to fake blush when hit on with such bad chat up lines.

"I'm looking for an expensive perfume for a special someone. Is there anything you'd recommend?"

"You could try this one." Sylvia picked up a vibrant red bottle shaped like a deformed apple and sprayed some of its contents onto a strip of paper.

"Would it be possible for you to spray some on yourself? You can't really tell what a fragrance is like until it's on the skin."

Sylvia sprayed some onto her wrist. Ricki gently took her hand into his. He held it like he was holding Shakespeare's First Folio.

"That's really special. Although not half as special as you."

Sylvia giggled. Apparently bad lines did indeed work on her.

*

At a coffee shop chain within Dubai airport, where expensive-looking furniture, and sacks of coffee beans went side by side and blues music played in the background giving it a faux bohemian feel, a barista with a complexion of white sand and eyes as blue and as cold as the Baltic, waited for Ricki to stop gazing and to order a coffee.

"Hi. Can I get a double espresso and your phone number please?" Ricki made a James Bond-like wink at Yelena.

"You can certainly have an espresso," Yelena coolly said, her voice matching her eyes.

"I have to try. What's your name?"

"What's yours?" Yelena began making a double espresso. The sounds of the grinding coffee beans aroused Ricki.

"Ricki Singh. Maybe you've heard of me?"

"Don't think so. Building football stadiums in Qatar?"

Ricki shook his head. "No. Where are you

from?"

"Russia."

"Don't you get Bollywood films in Russia?"

"Hollywood?"

"Bollywood. Indian films."

"I'm sure but I don't like that kind of dancing."

"Perhaps I can expand your cultural horizons sometime?"

"It's possible."

"But I still don't know your name."

"Yelena." She finished making the double espresso and handed it over to Ricki.

"That's an exquisite name. What's it mean?"

"It means shining light."

"That's beautiful. You must be very useful when there's a power cut, yaar?"

"And your name?"

"Ricki Singh means handsome, generous, wonderful, great actor."

"All that? I don't believe you."

"You'd have to spend a day with me to find out."

"Only a day?"

"Five minutes would be enough. When do you have your break?"

"Not for another couple of hours."

"That's a shame. Well, feel free to join me if you can." Ricki gave Yelena one of his award-winning smiles then took his double espresso over to a corner table. He opened his magazine to the exact page where there was a major interview with Ravi Puri.

"Ravi!"

*

After finishing his coffee and giving Yelena one more look that said, 'I want to fuck your brains out', Ricki rapidly departed, earphones on listening to his tunes on his iPhone. He rushed to the urinal. Having a double espresso after already having had a coffee had taken its toll on his bladder.

"I knew I was drinking way too much coffee." Ricki pulled up at a urinal and let loose. Ricki sang enthusiastically with his voice the equal of William Shatner, *"Babe, you gotta admit you're into my love."*

Out of Ricki's field of vision, Tony stealthily padded in and scanned the area. The toilet cubicles and the restroom itself were vacant besides Ricki. Tony locked the main door then sneaked up behind Ricki. Tony grabbed Ricki's head, twisting it, breaking it, Ricki's body dropping to the floor with a loud thud.

"Zai jian, Romeo. Now no one will forget you."

Tony dragged Ricki's body into a cubicle, locked the door and removed cash from Ricki's wallet. He nimbly climbed up over the cubicle partition then got out his mobile phone and dialled a number that was written on a piece of scrap paper. Once the number connected, he spoke into the phone,

"Gazpacho."

Meanwhile at Chhatrapati Shivaji International Airport, Mumbai…

Another first-class departure lounge where the sound of the finest porcelain cups could be heard embracing their saucers, an athletically built Indian man wearing an expensive looking summer suit, held a cheap plastic mobile phone to his ear. He switched it off, and slipped it into his Chanel jacket pocket.

A slender woman with a mocha coffee complexion and dressed in the latest Paris fashions, rushed over to him. "Ravi, come on. Our plane is waiting."

"I'm coming, Sonal," the dapper Ravi replied.

Ravi handed two flight tickets to Sonal who passed them to a check-in girl. He then discreetly dropped the mobile phone into a bin. The check-in girl handed back the tickets. Ravi and Sonal, arm in arm, joyfully proceeded through and boarded.

3

Hong Kong International Airport

In a toilet cubicle at Hong Kong airport, Tony reached behind and underneath the toilet. He removed a small sealed package that he unwrapped to find a Ruger Mark III 22.45 Threaded Barrel with suppressor. With its stainless steel barrel and polymer frame, it was Tony's preferred gun of choice – it just felt right in his hand. Tony closed his eyes and stroked the barrel. He let out an almost sexual sigh.

Eva Kovic, a leggy blonde with high cheekbones and a look that immediately told you what she did for a living, rushed away, teary-eyed, pulling along a black Rimowa suitcase and carrying a bulging LV bag with the odd bit of clothing spilling out.

A stringy haired guy with more tattoos on him than skin, reached out and grabbed her arm. He was dressed in a black T-shirt with the rock band name *The Soon Departed'* splashed across it.

"Get away from me, Zack," Eva pleaded. Her accent had a hint of New York, though was still heavily set in her birth country of Slovenia.

"Look, it's not like, I mean... You know I love you," Zack spluttered out. He was a much better guitarist than talker of words.

"Yeah, you love me. You love me so much that you slept with my best friend. Everyone warned me about you... Why didn't I listen?"

"Naomi's like nothing. She's a speck of... You're my oxygen, babe."

"She meant plenty when you screamed her name in our bed!"

"That's just sex, babe. Come on lighten up. It's the 21st century. This is totally not rock 'n' roll."

Eva slapped Zack hard across the face. So hard that it made his head turn a swift 90°. "My god, you're such an asshole!"

"You can't leave me. You've got my kid in there." Zack pointed at Eva's belly as though Eva was totally clueless about the birds and the bees.

"Not for much longer."

"Hey, don't I get a say? It's my sperm!"

"Please go. And tell that slut the next time I see her I'm going to make it so that she'll never be able to lift her legs over her head again."

Zack stroked Eva's arm. "Babe, don't do this. We've got history. You're my girl."

"And it is history. Anyway, I told my dad and brothers. If I were you, I wouldn't dream of coming back to Sydney."

Zack froze as Eva made her way to the Cathay Pacific first class departure lounge where Tony was surveying the elegant lounge with its deep-seated sofas, views overlooking the airport, muzak and clinking champagne flutes. Tony spotted a fidgeting and sweaty Japanese businessman who was wearing a pinstriped suit. The Japanese businessman was clutching onto a briefcase. Tony sat himself nearby when Eva brushed past. She dropped her LV bag and her belongings fell out. She knelt to pick her things up then broke down, crying uncontrollably.

"Let me help." Tony assisted Eva and gathered up her belongings then handed them over to Eva. "Do not cry. This is not so embarrassing. In Taipei, my ex-wife had to give birth inside a taxi during rush hour."

Eva put everything back into her bag.

"Please, have a seat. Can I get you something? Coffee? Tea? Whiskey?" Tony offered.

"Just a gun so I can kill my boyfriend. Ex-boyfriend." Eva accepted his offering of a seat.

Tony patted his jacket. "Now I remember. Security took it." Tony kept an eye on the Japanese businessman, who padded his forehead dry with a handkerchief. "Is that your boyfriend?" Tony pointed at Zack, who looked like a meerkat, as he poked his head over a seat.

"Jesus. He's like a two-timing homing pigeon."

"Eva! Babe!" Zack called out.

"I'm going to hide in the toilets." Eva left with Zack in hot pursuit.

Still clutching his briefcase, the Japanese businessman anxiously got up, looking to his left, to his right then scurrying away like a paranoid crab and made his way to a multi-faith prayer room. Tony followed, stealthily in hot pursuit and locked the door behind him. Tony delicately removed his handgun and attached the suppressor. The Japanese businessman knelt and bowed his head in prayer, completely oblivious to Tony's presence. Tony crept up behind him and fired off two headshots.

"Your friends wish you a pleasant onward journey." Tony emptied the Japanese businessman's wallet then hauled him off and hid him in a closet. He got out his mobile phone and made a call.

"Gazpacho… We meet as agreed… Don't worry about Mr Sakamoto. He won't be causing you any more problems."

Tony wandered back to the first class departure lunge and sat in the same seat as before. He put the briefcase down between his feet, letting it stick out a tad. Zack ran past and tripped over the briefcase, causing him to yelp in a rather high-pitched manner.

"What the fuck, man?" Zack shouted.

Tony tried helping Zack up but Zack brushed him off like the prima donna he was.

"You can't just leave your stuff there, man."

"I didn't," Tony said.

"I could've suffered some serious brain damage or something."

"I apologise."

"This brain's come up with some of the greatest songs since Jeff Buckley went under singing *Whole Lotta Love'*. Your bag could've totally broken every teenager's heart."

"You look familiar."

"I'm an international rock star, course I look familiar. Your daughter's probably got me on her wall, and in her dreams."

"There was a girl, tall..."

"You seen Eva? Where is she?"

"She said she was going to stay in Hong Kong and hang out with the pandas because they are more intelligent than her boyfriend."

Zack beat a hasty exit. Eva returned once it was all clear.

"I thought you were going to hide in the toilets," Tony said.

"Tried but somebody's got a severe case of the runs. Completely stunk the place out. I saw Zack with you. Which way did he go?"

"Back to Hong Kong to visit the pandas."

"Pandas? God, he's weird. I'm so sorry for getting you caught up in this."

"No problem. Nice distraction from work."

"What do you do? Relationship counsellor?"

"Travelling salesman. I buy cheap goods in a developing country and sell them at over inflated prices in developed ones."

"Been shopping?"

"The briefcase? I promised a friend I would get him one. He'd kill me if I didn't."

Eva's mobile rang. A Miley Cyrus ringtone. Eva's taste in boyfriends ran to music. "Ugh. It's Zack." She went over to a corner of the lounge, and massaged her forehead with the tips of her fingers whilst she spoke to Zack on her mobile. "How are the pandas? … What? … You really need to lay off the pot… I don't want to hear any more of your pathetic excuses… Don't tell me you love me. Go and tell it to your cheap whore." Eva hung up and re-joined Tony.

"Where is he?" Tony asked.

"On another planet."

"Then I think I see his double."

"Jesus." Eva shot up and was off like a bullet.

Zack hurried over to Tony. "Where's she gone? You lied to me, bro. That ain't cool."

"I was in a difficult position."

"You're messing with me. Maybe you don't get who you're fucking with? I know people, you know?"

"I understand."

"This is your last chance, Jackie. Now, where'd she go?" Zack shook a fist at Tony.

"Okay, okay. Just calm down, I don't want trouble. She said she was going to buy a handbag."

"Duh!" Zack slapped his own forehead. "Why didn't I think of that? Chicks love bags." Zack departed.

Eva re-emerged. "Where did you send him?"

"Shopping."

"I need a break. I feel like a fox being chased by a dim-witted hound. What's your name?"

"Patrick Li."

"Patrick Li, the salesman. What are you selling this time?"

"Books on erectile dysfunction."

"That's something Zack doesn't suffer from."

"One day it can happen."

Zack should get a vasectomy for the good of the world. You're going back home to Taipei? That's where you're from right?"

"From."

"Don't you live there anymore? Where do you call home?"

"Name any airport."

"Didn't you say you had a wife?"

"Ex."

"And a child?"

"I haven't seen him for a few years."

"I know I shouldn't ask, I mean it's none of my business but... Why not?"

"Sometimes when you love someone so much, you don't see them because you know you'd cause more problems if you were in their life."

"He must really miss you. What's his mum say?"

"She's happy. I'm no role model."

"I'm sure you're not that bad. I bet your son would love to know you."

"The less he sees me the less likely he'll become like me."

"Jeez, you're pretty down on yourself."

"I'm not down. I accept loneliness goes hand in

hand with my job."

"So, why do it?"

"It's only life I know and I'm good at it. If I didn't do this I'd be nothing instead of almost nothing."

"I hear that. If you're a model you're always on the road, unless you're not successful. Then you don't go anywhere."

"You seem quite nice but why were you and…"

"Why was I with Zack? I think it comes with the territory. Photo shoots and rock star boyfriends. What can I say? I wanted to be Kate Moss when I grew up."

"Babe!" Zack stood in front of Eva, his hands clasped together like he was pleading.

"Go away!"

"I had a moment like, it was all clear. I fucked up, you gotta forgive me. You're my destiny."

"I will leave you alone." Tony got up to go.

"Yeah, take a hike, Jet."

"Zack! Shut up. God, you're an idiot."

Zack grabbed Eva's arm but she wrestled free. Tony got in-between them and placed the tips of the fingers of his hand onto Zack's chest.

"See my fingers? In Wing Chun there is a move called the one-inch punch. Bruce Lee could break planks of wood doing this. Imagine the effect on you." Other passengers stopped what they were doing and watched on fascinated.

Zack's eyes were locked on Tony before he brushed Tony's hand away, laughing. "You almost had me there, Mr Miyagi. I'm outta here."

Eva waited as Zack stayed true to his word and got 'outta' there. "If you get fed up with being a salesman, maybe you could be a bodyguard… I have to get going. I'll catch you sometime at some other airport, Mr Li." Eva picked up her luggage and wandered into the main airport terminal, where Zack was leaning up against a wall out of Eva's eyesight.

"You can't blank me forever," Zack called out to Eva. He then caught up with her.

"It's pretty hard with you in my face all the time." Eva stood her ground. Getting away from him was proving impossible.

"We've shared time, years babe…"

"In the past, where you are."

"How can you say that? Show me the face that made me write *Let Me Roam in Your Love Valley*?"

"I hated that song. It was so 80s spandex."

Zack staggered back clutching his heart.

"It sucked more than your slut."

"I serenaded you with it at the SMA's!"

"Yes, and I've never been so embarrassed in front of 2,000 music industry people."

"You're a black magic woman and I'm your voodoo doll."

"Bye Zack."

Eva departed for the millionth time. Zack cut a forlorn figure.

"You've broken my heart," he said, head bowed. Then he waved his fist, "I'm gonna tweet this! You'll be replaced! There are thousands of 'Zackachicas' just waiting to step in."

Zack wandered like that lonely cloud and soon found himself plopping down next to a perplexed-looking Tony. Why would he sit next to him?

"It's over, Bruce. She dissed my song. There's no return." Zack got out his mobile and tweeted: 'ZackEva, romance of your time, is over. I am a free man. #Zackachicas now's your chance. #ZackNeedsBreakUpSex (no fatties)'. Zack put his mobile away then turned to Tony. "Dude? Do you really know how to do that one-inch punch thingy? Can you show me?"

"It takes a long time."

"I've always been a fast learner."

"I'm not a teacher."

"Come on! I'll pay."

"I don't need money."

"What is this, some kind of Chinese code that you can't teach a white dude? Tell you what, I'll meet your daughter."

"Don't have one."

"Look bro, just five minutes, alright?"

"Okay but not here."

"Sweet."

Tony led Zack to the multi-faith prayer room and closed the door behind them.

"You wanna do it in here? Ain't this a place of God or something?"

Tony locked the door.

"What you doing?" Zack queried with some understandable apprehension.

"Privacy. I don't want other Chinese people to know I'm teaching a gweilo this."

"Right, code of the prawn crackers or something. So, come on! What should I do?"

"Stand in front of me." Tony took out his gun and pistol-whipped Zack across the back of the head. Zack dropped like a sack of potatoes. Tony put on a black leather glove and pulled out Zack's wallet. He took out the cash and also found a packet of Viagra. He grinned then pocketed the Viagra as well. Tony wiped his gun then placed it into Zack's hands.

4

Narita International Airport, Tokyo

In a restroom of Narita International Airport with its granite floor and granite surfaces, an Argentinean with shoulder length pitch-black hair, washed his unshaven face. He had dark shadows under his eyes and looked older than his 25 years.

Daniel Cordoba, wearing his beloved crocodile skin boots that made a loud tap sound each time he walked, went into one of the cubicles and removed his designer T-shirt. His chest and upper arms were covered in narrow scars caused by self-inflicted knife wounds. Daniel took a plaster from his pocket and changed an old one on a recent wound.

At the same airport in the ladies' toilets, Eva headed to a cubicle. Before she reached it she saw a young mother changing her baby's nappy. Eva paused. Pain was evident across her face. In the cubicle, Eva held her head in her hands as she overheard the young mother make cute baby noises, which the baby responded to.

Under her breath Eva whispered, "Please shut up." Tears started building in her eyes, as she fought to regain control of her emotions.

In a duty-free shop Daniel browsed through the racks of mochi, and got a box of cocoa mochi. The cocoa mochi were dusted in powdered sugar. As he purchased the box he glanced up and saw Eva hugging goodbye another model – one that resembled Kate Moss in figure and face.

"Please God, let it be her. I will go to church, visit my sister and stop throwing cigarettes at that dog that pisses on my Vespa."

Daniel held onto his box of mocha. He took a seat in the first class departure lounge, with its mood lighting, granite table tops and wine bar to the side that served the finest sake. Eva flicked through a fashion magazine then left her seat and took one next to Daniel.

"Daniel?"

Daniel quickly turned away, and whispered under his breath, "Gracias!" He faced Eva. "Si. Hola. How are you?" Daniel leant in to kiss Eva on the cheek but she backed away. "I got the cocoa mochi. Would you like a piece?"

"I don't do sweets covered in powdered sugar, especially when I'm out in makeup."

"What do you do?"

"Nothing."

"You are going home?"

"Aha. Let's cut the chit-chat." Eva marched away with Daniel trying to keep up. With stealth that Tony would've been proud of, they sneaked into a disabled toilet then began ripping off each other's clothes and met in a passionate clinch.

"I have some coca..."

"Shut up. You got a rubber?"

"Right, right. Sure." Daniel grabbed one from his wallet. Eva headed back in for another steamy embrace.

*

Both looking somewhat dishevelled following

28

their passionate encounter, though Daniel was pretty dishevelled even before the sex, they sat themselves on bar stools at a chic bar at Narita Airport.

"Cosmopolitan," Eva ordered.

"Asahi. Make it two." Daniel swivelled on his stool. "Have you used that app before?"

"Nope."

"Me neither." Daniel lied. "I hope I was good. I got worried because I thought I saw you cry at one time and I was getting…"

"What's it like in Buenos Aires?"

"It is very seductive. The tango's in your step and the people are spicy. How long were you in Tokyo?"

A barman returned with their drinks and the bill. Eva and Daniel both made a grab for the bill.

"I want to pay for my drink," Eva said.

"No, no. I insist." Daniel took the bill away from her and paid.

"What did you ask?"

"You are somewhere else. Are you okay?"

"Fine."

"What were you doing in Tokyo? Partying?"

"Does it matter?"

"No, but, you know, after sex I like to talk. Normally I would smoke but there are regulations."

"Do you have a girlfriend back home?"

"I thought no personal information. This is the rule, no?"

"I have time before my flight. We can sit in silence, if you want? Actually, maybe I should go…"

"Wait, wait. No girlfriend." Daniel knocked back some of his beer. "No one who will miss me. Who's Zack?"

"What?"

"You call out his name."

"He's no one. An ex."

"I feel like this is a little unfair. You know my name and that I'm from Buenos Aires. All I know about you is that you have an ex called Zack."

"You got laid by a model, isn't that most guys' dream? What are you complaining about?"

"Call me old-fashioned, but if I have sex with a girl, I like to know a little about her. Especially passionate sex."

"That wasn't passion."

"You seemed pretty passionate to me."

"It was anger."

"Why are you angry?"

"Why are you asking?"

Daniel knocked back more of his beer till less than a quarter remained. Man, he was thirsty! "Now I know why that app is called BriefEx."

Eva checked her Cartier watch. "I was in Tokyo having an abortion. It was for the best."

"Whoa. Did you tell Zack?"

"Unfortunately. The asshole's addicted to Twitter."

Daniels brain finally clicked into gear. "Wait. Zack? From *The Soon Departed*? You're Eva Kovic?"

A look of shock hit Eva's face like lightning had just missed her.

"I'm a music journalist." He wanted to stand up on the bar and shout out that he'd just fucked Eva Kovic.

"Fuck." Eva leapt to her feet.

Daniel grabbed her hand. "What are you doing? Where are you going?"

"This was meant to be anonymous, and now look - you know all about me. I can't believe I did this... and with a fucking journalist."

"Even journalists do it. But listen, I am not Zack. I will not tweet this or tell anybody. Come on sit down. Please."

Eva retook her seat then pulled out a tissue from her bag.

"I think you did the right thing leaving him. I know his kind."

"Of course you do - you're a guy. You think with your dick. And you're Latino, so that probably goes double."

"I admit that hot, fiery passion streams through this body but when I am with a girl, I do not fuck around. Never."

"You're a liar. I bet when you fancy someone else, you dump your girlfriend then fuck the new one in the old one's bed. You're all alike."

"Jesus. Not all men are boludos. I had a girlfriend. Paola. We broke up three years ago. But when we were together, there was no one else."

"Did you love her?"

"I proposed."

"But you didn't get married?"

"My father caused many problems."

"What did your father have to do with it?"

"You do not know him. She was great. Even my Mama liked her and she's very picky. No girl was good enough for Mama's Danielito."

"Was Paola a good Catholic girl?"

"In comparison to my other girlfriends, Paola was like a nun. That's why Mama liked her. She was just about Catholic enough for her."

"Must be difficult to find someone with such a dominant family around you. My mum and dad have always been easy with who I've been with. Maybe too easy. I think I'll be a lot stricter if I become a mum."

"Then you have to find a man."

"I'd rather have a dog and the address of a sperm bank."

"But then you do not know who you're getting."

"Exactly. Leave it to me to find a sperm donor and I'd end up getting knocked up by the missing link."

"What is a missing link?"

"Someone like Zack."

"You could get a missing link from a sperm bank too."

"But there's also a chance I could get a doctor's."

"You will get over it and find someone new. Just maybe avoid anyone in music."

"Yeah, right. You're the first guy I've been with and look at what you do... It's like I'm a magnet to guys in the industry."

"My uncle lives in Chacras de Coria, a few kilometres from Mendoza. I guarantee that if you lived there you will not find anybody involved in music. You might meet a winegrower."

"I love wine."

"Argentinian?"

"Don't care. Cigarettes and alcohol."

"Tobacco's cheap too."

"Maybe I'll make it my next stop."

"You could stay with me."

"I don't think your mama would like me. I'd be the Sinner to Paola's Saint."

"Mama would not meet you."

"Would you hide me in your cellar?"

"She died a few years ago."

"In your cellar?"

"Beautiful. You're joking about my mother."

Eva tenderly put her hand on his leg. She'd gone too far. "I'm sorry. How'd she die? If you don't mind my asking."

"Cancer. Years of stress and abuse from my father."

"You blame him?"

"No need to."

There was an announcement over the tannoy, "Passengers for Qantas flight QF22 to Sydney. Please proceed to gate 18."

"We've still got a few minutes." Eva placed a hand onto Daniel's knee.

"Is that a hint?"

"A hint so huge that there's a giant, flashing neon sign that reads, 'this is a hint'."

Eva and Daniel got up and hurried away to the nearest disabled toilets.

"Hey, you know, when we get to Sydney, perhaps we could see each other?"

They passed a television monitor and stopped, frozen, eyes glued to the screen. On the screen, Zack's handcuffed, struggling with the police as he's taken out of a police van.

"Zack Jones, lead singer of the band 'The Soon Departed', was charged today with the murder of Japanese businessman, Yosuke Sakamoto," said a news reporter.

Eva pinched the bridge of her nose then ran her hand through her hair. Her eyes were wide, as was her mouth. "Holy fuck!"

5

Sydney-Kingsford Smith International Airport

In a generic airport seating area with metal seats not meant to be sat in for more than a few minutes, Daniel was sweating, and his eyes darted around feverishly as he started coming down from his latest high.

Just across from Daniel, a bearded gentleman in his late 50s, clad in a tweed blazer, studied a medical journal. Occasionally, he shot an appraising look towards Daniel, studying him like he was trying to solve Fermat's last theorem.

Daniel's father, Señor Cordoba, joined Daniel next to him. Señor Cordoba was in his late 60s, had a wine belly from years of consuming red wine and having sausage to go with it. His lack of hair was not due to either of those things, however. Señor Cordoba berated Daniel in his husky, deep Argentinian voice that could've scared children and melted stone.

"Daniel! Daniel!" Señor Cordoba started.

"Huh?" Daniel was perplexed and confused.

"You're my biggest mistake. You should've been strangled at birth."

"What?"

"Look what you've become! A nothing. A junky, a useless drug addict."

"It's not true."

"Yes, it is. You can't even look yourself in the mirror because of your shame. Even that girl would rather be with her no good boyfriend than a junky like you."

"Shut up."

"You only have that job because of me and look at the shit job you're doing."

"I'm trying."

"You've never been good at anything. Not like your sister. I'm embarrassed to call you my son."

"Stop."

"I tell people now that you're not mine. My real son is dead. Why don't you do us all a favour and end your pathetic life?"

"Shut up!"

A couple of middle-aged passengers seated near to Daniel glanced at him. Daniel rushed away to the nearest toilets then splashed water over his face hoping it would refresh him. He stared in the mirror and wiped away the water. Señor Cordoba re-appeared behind him.

"Look at you."

"Why don't you fuck off, you miserable shit?"

"No respect."

"Like you are so great. If I'm such a shit, then just look who I came from! Whatever I am it's because of you. That's what makes you angry, is that you created me. We're the same."

"No. We're not the same, Daniel. I made something of my life."

"Did you? You had it easy. You didn't have a father who beat his wife and children. You didn't have a father who killed his son's mother."

"You, you fucking had it easy. Had everything given to you on a plate. I came to Buenos Aires with nothing and built myself up from scratch."

"You try to make yourself sound like you're

something special but you are nothing. Just a cheating, woman beater."

"Without me around, you'd just be some worthless, homeless junky. Thanks to me, you're just a junky."

"Yeah, because of you. Now leave me alone."

"Pathetic, waste of..."

"I said, 'leave me alone!'"

Daniel smashed the mirror in front of him and dropped to the floor in a crumpled heap. Leaning up against the wall he clasped his head in his hands. His mother, Mama Cordoba, appeared in front of him wearing her famed tight flowery dress, looking particularly good for 40 something. She used to smell of lilac, and with her mahogany complexion she was the envy of all of Daniels friends' mothers, and the reason why his friends always went to his house. She crouched down next to him.

"Danielito."

"Mama."

"Don't listen to him, Daniel."

"Mama, I need you."

"Be strong, I'm always with you." Mama Cordoba cradled Daniel.

"Don't go. Please." Daniel broke down. Through his teary eyes he saw that the arm around him wasn't his mother but that of the bearded gentleman who'd been sitting across from him.

"Hello."

*

Looking decidedly refreshed, Daniel sipped a mineral water at a chain-style coffee shop. Daniel's cut hand was bandaged up.

"Thanks for doing my hand."

"Think nothing of it." The bearded chap spoke with a thick Austrian accent.

"What's your name?"

"Dr Franz Krugman but you can call me Franz. How are you feeling?"

"Better, thank you. I'm sorry about before."

"It's fine. Sometimes we have these moments. What made you smash the mirror?" Franz added two packets of brown sugar into his espresso then stirred.

"I don't know. Just did."

"Are you taking anything right now?"

"You mean like prescription drugs?"

"Yes, or other more recreational substances." Daniel shied away.

"Don't worry Daniel, I'm not the police."

"I do some things."

"I can't judge you, God knows I've experimented in my time. Just take it easy. Who were you talking to in there?"

"It's embarrassing."

"Go on, you can tell me."

"I was talking to my mother. Sometimes I see her and we talk."

"Where is she now? Buenos Aires?"

"In a way."

"And your father?"

"He *lives* in Buenos Aires, unfortunately."

"You don't get along?"

"Never. Imagine a chainsaw on steel. Sparks will fly."

"That's not unusual. My father and I never saw eye to eye."

"Me and dad are complete opposites. As a kid I used to question whether we were blood. I was 99% sure my mama had had an affair. Not that she ever could or would have done. That kind of disappointed me."

"Isn't there a chance of reconciliation?"

"I think there is more possibility of finding intelligent life on Mars."

"That's a shame, especially for your father. As he gets older he'll regret not healing the rift with you."

"It'll be on his conscience."

"Unfortunately, it'll be on yours too."

"I can live with it. I've done my best. He's the fuck up."

"Is he the reason why you turned to drugs?"

"Haven't you ever needed to escape from an indescribable pain?"

"Yes, many times, but I chose not to hurt myself. If someone were causing me pain why would I take it out on myself?"

"What do you mean?"

"I mean I cure the problem at the root." Franz gulped down his espresso.

"Some roots are long and tangled and not so easy to straighten out."

"Nothing's too difficult. You just make the call and, like magic, the problem's gone."

"That easy?"

"Why not? Life is easy to change, we only think that it's not."

"Even if it's a blood relation?"

"Sure, especially if that blood is poisoned. You know Daniel, bullies are inconsequential in the long run."

"What do you do, Franz?"

"I'm an intermediary."

"Meaning?"

"I'm a link between a problem and its solution."

"Like a weed killer?"

"More like a mail order catalogue selling weed killer. Sometimes, the law and the judicial system are useless. Nothing is solved, or it takes an inordinate amount of time. So I built up a network of people that stretches from Mexico City to London, from Johannesburg to Taipei. People who perform quick solutions."

"You ship far and wide."

"And we always deliver." Franz checked the airport monitors. "I think it's time to go for our flight."

"You know, Franz, I'm going to stay in Sydney for a few more days."

"What about Buenos Aires?"

"It just feels too soon. I need a few days before I go back."

"Yes, maybe that's a good idea."

"And there's a girl here that I... well, she's making a big mistake."

"Good luck to you, Daniel."

"You too, Franz."

Franz and Daniel shook hands then parted ways. Franz headed towards a newsagents whilst talking on his mobile.

"The seed's been sown… Returning now. Should I give the word? …Wire the rest on completion."

At the newsagent, Franz picked up a tabloid newspaper and an entertainment magazine. He went to the till and took out his wallet. As he removed AUD20 from his wallet and handed it to the young female cashier, his eyes lingered upon a photo in his wallet. The photo showed him holding hands with a warm, yet fragile-looking woman in her late 40s, though she looked older and had lost most of her hair. The woman's lying in a hospital bed.

"Sir?" the young female cashier said.

Franz snapped out of it. "Yes?"

"Your change." The cashier gave Franz his change. Franz removed the photograph, and as he left the shop he scrunched it up and dropped it into a bin.

6

Ministro Pistarini International Airport, Buenos Aires

A freshly brewed pot of coffee stood on a table between two leather sofas in a secluded corner of the comfortable departure lounge at the Ministro Pistarini International Airport. Franz poured two cups of coffee, the other for Ana Maria Alvarez, a 31 year-old with a Penelope Cruz face and a Salma Hayek body. She sat, cross-legged in her high heels, chic black outfit, $500 sunglasses, and long black hair tied straight back as if she were in mourning.

"Cream?" Franz then added cream to both cups of coffee. "I'm sorry that I couldn't meet you in Caracas."

Ana Maria had a severe case of the fidgets. "Any excuse to leave Venezuela right now. I wish I could smoke in these places." She got out her chrome-plated lighter and fiddled with it. "You know about my situation?"

"Completely."

"So you also know what the media say about me?"

"I'm afraid so, yes."

Ana Maria removed an A4 manila envelope from her stylish black and gold handbag. She slid it across to Franz. "I have all the information in here."

Franz peered inside the envelope. "This is quite unusual."

"I know, but I hope it can be done."

Franz stroked his hairy grey-haired chin. He had

the look and personality of a psychiatrist as everything and everybody was worthy of observation and analysis – one or two lumps of sugar in his coffee required at least 20 seconds of consideration. Heck, he was the spitting image of Sigmund Freud. "I never normally ask, but are you sure?"

"I'm paying a lot of money for that question not to be asked."

"Once I make the arrangements, there's no going back."

"That's not a problem."

"I read that you have a son."

"Don't bring him into this."

"Have you thought how this might affect him?"

Ana Maria removed her sunglasses revealing dark shadows under her eyes like she hadn't slept in weeks. "Of course I've considered it. I didn't just decide overnight. So, you will do it?"

"I have some reservations."

"Fuck." Ana Maria threw her hands to her head then rummaged through her handbag and grabbed a pack of cigarettes. With her hands trembling, she eventually lit one, taking frequent puffs. "You want more money?"

"It's not a question of money as such."

"Of course it is. It always is. I can pay more."

A waiter came over. "I'm sorry, madam, there is a non-smoking policy."

"Fuck. Get me an ashtray or a saucer…"

The waiter fetched a saucer. Ana Maria put out her cigarette. Franz waited for the waiter to leave.

"Señora Alvarez, we only take on jobs where the risk is far outweighed by the reward."

"Can't you see I'm desperate? Please Dr

Krugman, help me."

Franz sighed. "I'll see what I can do." He got up, offered his hand to Ana Maria then departed.

Ana Maria finished a bit more of her coffee before heading away. She passed a table with a middle-aged couple at it. They pointed and spoke in hushed tones. Ana Maria quickened her step and made her way to a swanky, upmarket bar in the airport. She had with her a Venezuelan newspaper. She again opted for a corner table, wishing to remain as hidden as possible. A stylish-looking waiter promptly came to her table to take her order.

"Gin and tonic," Ana Maria ordered.

A sharp-suited businessman started staring at Ana Maria.

"What? What are you looking at?"

The businessman held up his hands up to plead, 'no offence'. The waiter returned with her gin and tonic.

"Gracias." She opened up the newspaper, *La Voz de Mañana*'. Her eyes become transfixed on the front-page headline *'Ana Maria Alvarez envuelta en un escándalo sexual!'* A censored photo showed a naked Ana Maria lying with a 25-year-old curvaceous woman, and a dark-haired, muscular Pablo Vazqued – a guy quite similar in looks to Marlon Brando when he appeared in *'A Streetcar Named Desire'*.

Pablo himself then showed up, wearing a $2000 designer suit, though he made it look even more expensive. He was the epitome of a Fancy Dan or a flash harry.

"Pablo? What are you doing here?" Ana Maria wanted to smoke again.

"I've been looking everywhere for you."

"Why?"

"You left so quickly, you didn't give me a chance to speak with you."

"Couldn't you have called me instead of following me to Buenos Aires?"

"I tried but you wouldn't answer."

"What do you expect?"

"So now you see why I had to come in person."

"No, I don't. What if someone spots us?"

"Stop this paranoia. No one's going to be watching."

"Are you crazy?" Ana Maria shoved the *La Voz de Mañana'* newspaper in front of Pablo. She scrunched up her fist and clenched her teeth. "All of Venezuela has seen a sex tape of you, me and Ramona. My life's over and you think I'm paranoid?" Ana removed her sunglasses. There was a sadness in her eyes that even an overdose of happiness wouldn't have been able to rectify.

"Ana, that's why we need to talk."

"We have nothing to talk about. All you care about is your singing and nothing else."

"Of course I care about my career. Don't you?"

"Why should I? I've lost Jorge, my family and my son. Nothing else matters."

"Have you seen Juanito?"

"Jorge won't let me."

"He can't stop you seeing your son."

"Don't be stupid, Pablo."

"I can help you get Juanito."

"What can you do? Jorge was already filing for divorce before this tape. He's known about us for a long time."

"How could he?"

"Just go, please. I need to be alone." Ana Maria played with her hair. She wanted the ground to open and swallow her up.

"No. Ana, we can get through this if we stick together."

"If I want Juanito, the last thing I need is to be seen with you."

"Do you know how *'La Voz de Mañana'* got this tape?"

"Didn't you give it to them?"

"How can you say that?"

"You couldn't resist telling the world what a playboy you are. Men will envy you, women will love you, and I'll just be a slut."

"My name is mud too."

"Oh come on, we're Catholic. I'm the one who's either the Madonna or the Whore."

"Look, maybe it will die down."

"I was the biggest star in Latin America. Why did I do it?"

"We were drunk."

"And you think that's a good excuse?"

"What do you want from me? It's not my fault what happened."

"I just want you to leave me alone and try and forget what happened."

Pablo moved closer to Ana and held her arm. "Now who's crazy? This isn't going to go away, we've got to face it and..."

"And what?"

"We're the hottest thing in Venezuela. My music's in the top ten on iTunes. I have every talk show host wanting to interview me."

"I'm very happy that everything's so good for

you. Your career was always the most important thing to you."

"Don't you understand, Ana? This could be great for us."

"How? I won't even be able to show my face in public again. I don't know how you can feel no shame." Her voice was shaky.

"You're only ashamed because you got caught and now everyone can watch what you did."

"What's going to happen when Juanito's older and sees what his mother is?"

"You can't feel guilty about this. You did what you wanted to do..."

"In private. Why did this happen? I'm going to lose him." Ana Maria reached for her lighter.

"You're a good mother. He'll get over it."

"No, he won't."

"Why did you come to Buenos Aires?"

"Do you want to tell *La Voz de Mañana*' that too?"

"I didn't give them the tape. So, what will you do?"

"I must speak to my agent."

"My agent said if I apologise then it will be okay."

"For you."

"Maybe for us. Honestly Ana, I don't think it will be that bad."

"How can you say that? My father won't speak to me. I'm dead to my family. This thing is all over the Internet."

"Give it time. People will forget."

"I don't believe you." Ana Maria checked her watch. "I have to go. I have a flight." Ana Maria tried walking away as Pablo tugged at her arm.

"Stay with me through this." Pablo said with the utmost sincerity.

"Pablo, I don't want anything to do with you again."

Hidden inside a nearby café Franz watched Ana Maria hurrying away from Pablo. He took out his mobile.

"She's leaving now… Do you want me to proceed as planned? … Very well." Franz hung up.

7

Benito Juçrez International Airport, Mexico City

At a contemporary restaurant with brown-coloured upholstered booths, red-cloth upholstered chairs, soft lighting and the best of Mexican cuisine, Ana Maria hid behind sunglasses at one of the secluded booths. Sharing her table was her American agent, Vicky Steinberg, short in stature but big in personality. Vicky's shoulder length strawberry blonde hair, her choice of business suits and her Botoxed reinforced lips signalled a personality that was tough – she was not a person to trifle with. A strict Jewish upbringing with a battle-axe of a mother guaranteed that she'd develop into an offstage version of Joan Rivers.

Vicky munched loudly on a Caesar salad, ignoring all the public eating rules, as Ana Maria religiously stirred her iced-tea.

"Had you been seeing Pablo for long?" Vicky asked between crunchy mouthfuls.

"Several months, I guess. What's happening in America?"

"It's pretty big, honey. You want some of my salad? It needs more Parmesan."

"My career's over." Ana Maria sunk, inside and out. Her head drooped, so did her heart. What was to become of her?

"I'm doing all I can. I've got an interview set up."

"I don't think I can do it."

"Don't worry, honey, she's a friend of mine.

She'll write a good piece. I have a lot of contacts in the media."

"What does it matter when everybody hates me?"

"Don't jump the gun just yet. This is a new story. Anything could happen."

"What do you mean?"

"Have a little faith in your agent. I spoke to Jorge."

"What did he say? Can I see Juanito?"

"Not yet. He needs time."

"He won't ever let me see him again."

"He's very angry but he still loves you. Don't worry, honey. I got to get another spritzer." Vicky stuck her hand up and hailed a waiter over. The waiter promptly came. "I'm dying of thirst here. Go get me another spritzer… and this Caesar salad is like a dairy-free zone! Lashings of more Parmesan, please!" The waiter took away her half-eaten bowl of salad.

"How do you know he still loves me?"

"You could hear it in his voice. And he told me." She washed a mouthful of salad down with ice water.

"Even if he loves me, he'll never forgive me."

"I think he will. Give it time, honey."

"No. He was already trying to divorce me."

"You're going to have to speak to him about that. Listen, you'll need to release a statement."

"Vicky, I cannot."

"You've got to trust me, Ana. How long have we known each other? We're going to fight this together. By the time it's over, I'll have you smelling like a rose." Vicky's spritzer arrived along with her Caesar salad now covered in shavings of Parmesan.

"What should I say?"

"Don't worry, honey. I'll write it for you."

"When do you want me to do it?"

"Not yet. When the time comes I'll set it up. We'll also get you to donate to some charities, like a women's shelter or some starving kids thing."

"What about my music? My album?"

"I spoke to your label and it's all on hold. Your album, your tour, the whole enchilada."

"And my movie?"

"That too, honey. Right now we have to play the waiting game and see how all this plays out."

"I feel so violated. It's like my body isn't mine anymore but belongs to all of Venezuela."

"Try to be strong."

"I can't go back to Caracas. I just don't know how I can. I have to go to the restroom."

"You alright, honey? You're looking paler than a Goth that ain't seen sunshine in a year."

"I'll be okay."

Ana Maria went to the toilet and threw up what little she'd eaten that day. She flushed it all away. If only she could flush this story away and Pablo with it. She made her way to the sink and splashed water on her face hoping not only to revitalise herself but bring her colour back. Juanito must come back to her. Her son's rightful place was by his mother's side.

"Juanito."

Ana Maria rummaged through her handbag and got out some paracetamol and knocked back a couple of tablets. She took a few breaths then returned to Vicky. The table had been cleared except for a newly arrived cappuccino into which Vicky was emptying five sachets of sugar. Vicky gently touched Ana Maria's arm in an effort to reassure.

"It's going to be all right, honey. Trust me."

"I just want to get back to Jorge and Juanito. I miss them so much."

"What about Pablo? Didn't you love him?"

"No. I don't know why it happened. Excitement, I guess. It was just all so stupid. I don't even like him that much."

"I think it's time you returned home." Vicky tapped Ana Maria's arm then stuck her hand in the air again, and shouted, 'Check!"

*

Back at Ministro Pistarini International Airport, Buenos Aires, Pablo browsed the newspapers and magazines. He picked up *'La Voz de Mañana'* and skimmed through it. One of the pages he skimmed through had a small article with the headline, *'Detienen a argentino con drogas en el aeropuerto de Sydney'* – (Argentine arrested at Sydney airport for possession of drugs).

Pablo put the *'La Voz de Mañana'* back onto the shelf then grabbed a Spanish language women's magazine. Splashed on the front cover was his affair with Ana Maria.

He sniggered, "Gold mine."

*

It's night time in Mexico and Ana Maria's fully reclined on a black, leather armchair in the first class departure lounge at Benito Juçrez International Airport in Mexico City. She kissed a photo showing a bespectacled, debonair 30-something man with his arms wrapped around her, as Ana Maria held in her arms a two-year-old baby boy.

*

At an airport coffee shop Tony, dressed in his favourite blue Hawaiian shirt, peeked into an A4 manila envelope.

*

In Buenos Aires at a departure lounge, Pablo lay curled up on a sofa, a courtesy blanket covering him.

*

Tony splashed water on his face while at an airport restroom. He stared into the mirror, losing himself for a moment. There was someone else reflected in the mirror.

8

Simón Bolívar International Airport, Caracas

It was 9am the next day. At a waiting room in the airport, Ana Maria sat alone. She nibbled on her nails then got out her Max Factor compact and hurriedly touched up her face. A bespectacled, debonair chap from the photo Ana Maria had kissed breezed in, carrying a sleeping, olive-skinned infant. Ana Maria dropped everything.

"Jorge!" Ana Maria rushed into Jorge's embrace. United as a family, she took Juanito into her arms and smothered him in kisses, waking him up. The baby wasn't happy.

A while later at a conference room in the airport, Ana Maria, Jorge and Vicky appeared before a couple of dozen photographers, journalists and television crews in what seemed like a ravenous feeding frenzy of hyenas and vultures. Flash bulbs constantly went off creating a firework-like effect. Ana Maria slumped in a hunched position, her face free of sunglasses as she'd been told that it could come across as though she had something to hide. She'd resisted but Vicky had been persuasive. A bunch of microphones were stacked together like a bouquet of flowers; they offered a sort of paradoxical refuge. Jorge clutched her hand, trying to transfer some much needed courage.

Ana Maria, in a slightly more audible voice than the Korean Air princess, spoke meekly yet sincerely, "With all my heart, I would like to thank everyone for their support, especially my beautiful son and husband.

I'm looking forward to going home."

Vicky piped up. "Señora Alvarez won't be answering any questions."

Ana Maria and Jorge were leaving the media circus when a tubby middle-aged journalist who was probably only a few years away from his first heart bypass, raised a hand.

"Señora Alvarez? Are you going to sue Señor Pablo Vazqued?"

Vicky jumped in and fielded the question. "First we'll let the police carry out their investigation and then we'll consider our position."

The same journalist asked another, "Señora Alvarez, how do you feel about the police finding date rape drugs in Señor Vazqued's possession?"

"I'm sure you all appreciate that Señora Alvarez would like to be left alone with her family, and she asks that you respect her wishes. Thank you." Vicky ushered Ana and Jorge away.

At an exclusive lounge in the airport, reserved for VIPs, and away from the prying eyes of journalists greedy for salacious material, Ana Maria perused the front page of the *'La Voz de Mañana'* newspaper, smiling at the photo of a handcuffed Pablo being taken away by police. He looked bewildered and enraged.

The headline read, *Pablo Vazqued: ¿Traficante de drogas y chantajista?'* or, in English, *'Pablo Vazqued: Drug dealer and blackmailer?'*.

"Still, I cannot believe it. Trafficking drugs too?" Ana Maria kept shaking her head. She put the paper down.

Jorge massaged Ana Maria's shoulders then kissed the top of her head. She reached back and stroked his hand.

"It's over now, Ana. We can start again."

Ana Maria got up and hugged and kissed Jorge.

"I don't know about you but I need a drink. Would you like something?"

Jorge shook his head as she headed away to a well-stocked bar filled with an assortment of wines and spirits. Jorge hit dial on his mobile phone. The other end answered.

"Dr Franz Krugman? … I've wired through the rest of the money…" Jorge gazed at Ana Maria as she happily and with great delight made herself a gin and tonic. There was a renewed zest about her. "No, she doesn't suspect a thing."

9

Los Angeles Airport

At a Starbucks at LAX, with its rich coffee, lightly roasted beans and unique décor, a nineteen year-old blue-eyed boy in leather boots, and with hair associated with surfers from the 1991 movie, *'Point Break'*, Ashley Lee looked every bit the baked bean in a sea of green beans. He straightened out his red, cowboy checked shirt then went back to fidgeting with an empty plastic cup.

Ashley spoke in a voice that was a bit country and a bit Keanu Reeves. "Ma'am, I just want to thank you for meeting me. Ma'am? Miss Steinberg, I really appreciate you coming to meet me. Mrs Steinberg thanks for answering my letter… Ms Steinberg?" Ashley coughed. "Miss Steinberg?"

Vicky approached confidently, a woman on a mission, speaking authoritatively on her mobile phone while clutching a steaming cup of coffee that had been bought at a rival coffee shop.

"I don't care what Tom's getting, we want 18 mil. End of discussion." Vicky abruptly hung up then plopped down across from Ashley, who shifted uneasily. "So, you must be Ashley Lee."

"Yes ma'am. Ashley Lee from Buffalo, Wyoming."

"Where's your Stetson?"

"Sorry, ma'am?"

"You've been pestering my office for quite a while now."

"Yes ma'am, I have. I'm no quitter."

"So it seems. Too much perseverance can

become annoying. Be careful."

"I'll take that on board, ma'am."

"Stop calling me ma'am."

"Sorry ma'am, Miss Steinberg. Miss Steinberg: The best actor should have the best agent in Hollywood and I'm a great actor."

"Confidence is a good thing but over confidence is not."

"I reckon to make it in this town you can never have enough."

"So Ashley, why should I take you on?"

"Well, as I was saying, I'm a great actor and I reckon I could become as good as Robert De Niro."

"Hold on, Bob."

"Who's Bob?"

Vicky's mobile phone rang and vibrated. Her ringtone was the Mamas and the Papas' *California Dreamin'*. She answered. "Yes, Brian? … What? … No, tell them that Christina's got to have top billing or she's out of the picture… I don't care." Vicky abruptly hung up. "Why don't people listen? So, as good as Robert De Niro? How are you going to deal with constant rejection?"

"I'll keep at it. Nothing's gonna stop me."

"Because that's what Hollywood's about. It's about developing a tough façade. Taking the highs with the lows."

"Well, I don't plan on having too many lows, Miss Steinberg."

"Mrs."

"Mrs."

"You have to seize your chances here because if you don't, there are thousands waiting to replace you."

"Believe me, Mrs Steinberg, I'm ready. My

whole life, I've been waiting for this chance."

"Whole life? Aren't you 19?"

"Yes I am."

"I looked at your résumé. A few local television shows, nothing special."

"I know, ma'am. There's like not many chances for actors in Wyoming."

"I don't normally accept unknown actors. However, your tape was quite compelling."

"Does this mean you'll take me on?"

"Possibly. I'm not guaranteeing representation."

"It's half-way there and that's a hell of a lot further than I've got with any agent before."

"I'll get you to come by the office and sign a contract."

"Mrs Steinberg, I'm like blown away." Ashley got up and went to hug Vicky before she held her hands up in a 'please don't' gesture. He didn't know what to do. He puffed out his cheeks, looked around and considered breaking out in dance.

"Calm down, Ashley don't get your hopes up. We're still a long way from that."

Ashley retook his seat. "Whatever it is that you want me to do, I'll do it. You have no idea how much this means to me, Mrs Steinberg."

"Oh, I think I do. I have a friend whose husband's a director. He's making a new movie and he's about to hold auditions."

"That would be like, so awesome. I won't let you down."

"Slow down, Bobby, slow down. It just so happens that he's looking for kids like you."

"Why? Is he making a cowboy movie or something?"

Vicky's mobile rang again. "Steinberg… Nathaniel, darling! How are you? … I'm super… Don't you worry, I solved the problem for you. The bun no longer exists… She kicked up a stink but she won't be talking to anyone now. Your rep's as safe as the gold in Fort Knox… You're welcome… Yes, of course. We'll do dinner next week. Okay, ciao." Vicky gulped down some more of her coffee. No Starbuck employee had yet come over to Vicky telling her that she wasn't allowed to drink Coffee Bean and Tea Leaf coffee at a Starbucks. "So, you want to go to New York?"

"New York?"

"Yes, cowboy, it's a big city on the east coast."

"Whoa, New York. I've never been there. When's he want me?"

"I think he wants you pretty soon. Thursday at the latest."

"This Thursday?"

"The movie business moves fast. You either run with it or get run over."

"Can my girlfriend come?"

"This isn't a chance for a romantic vacation. You're trying to get a role in a movie, not get laid."

"Who's the director?"

"Nicholas Briddick. He's in New York till Friday morning then he flies back to London."

"Nicholas Briddick! Man, I like, so love his movies. Shit! Tell him I'll be there."

"Good. I'll get my assistant to arrange the flight then call you."

"Whoa, Nicholas Briddick. Where am I gonna stay?"

"Don't worry, it'll all be arranged. Are you sure you're ready for this?"

"You bet your ass! Never been as ready for anything in like all my life."

"I'm ecstatic to hear it."

"What kind of movie is it?"

"Nicholas was sketchy over the phone."

"Should I do anything for the audition, like learn something or...?"

"I've sent him your tape. I think he just wants you to do it cold."

"He saw my tape? Man, I can't believe it. He's seen my acting and he like, liked what he saw?"

"I expect you to listen to Nicholas and do what he says. A man of his experience and background, you could learn a lot." Vicky's mobile rang again. It was an important number.

"I sure will."

"Okay, must dash." Vicky sprung up from the table and departed with a better start than Usain Bolt. "I'm on my way… What? … No, it's served cold." Vicky was gone.

Ashley pumped a euphoric fist in the air. "Yeah!"

A short while later and Ashley was at a fast food chain, let's say Jack in the Box, sharing a strawberry milkshake with his girlfriend. His girlfriend was just 18, curvaceous, had bushy-haired blonde and wore tight denim. A silver necklace hung from around her neck.

"Ugh! Strawberry..." Ashley almost spat it out.

"I can't get ready to go to New York in two days!"

"Actually, Jen, I'm going alone. I'm sorry. I tried like real hard to get you a ticket but she said there's like no way."

"But I wanna go too!" Jennifer pouted then

bowed her head. Officially she was 18, but occasionally she came across as if she was only 13. She fiddled with her necklace.

"Hey, listen up. If I get this part, I'll be able to take us to New York every weekend. Don't be sad, alright? I thought you'd be happy for me."

"I am, it's just that you're going to get this part and like become a big Hollywood star and then forget about me."

"I'm never going to forget about you. You're always gonna be my girl."

"I won't. You'll have all those Hollywood women all over you. I'll be stuck in Wyoming working at a Bob Juniors, serving refills to creepy truckers on Interstate 90."

"That's not gonna happen." Ashley held Jennifer's hand.

"You promise?"

"Yeah. Now, we gotta move. Vicky's gonna call to confirm my flight."

"You're flying?"

"Duh! How'd you think I'm going to get to New York by Thursday?"

"You've never flown before."

"I better get used to it, you know. I'm gonna be flying all over the world soon."

"I'm really happy for you, Ash."

"I told you I was gonna make it."

"But if you're in New York, what am I going to do?"

"I'm only there for two days then I'll be back. Chill at the beach, check out Hollywood. Jesus, you're in LA!"

Ashley and Jennifer clutched each other's hands

then left the Jack in the Box. She stopped and pulled him back to face her.

"Wait. I want to give you something." Jennifer unhooked her necklace and tenderly put it into Ashley's hand. "I want you to have it. For good luck and so you won't forget me."

"I can't wear this."

"You don't have to wear it. Just keep it."

"But like your grandmother gave this to you."

"Yeah and now I want you to have it. Promise me you'll keep it always?"

"I will."

"Promise!" She tightened her grip on his hand.

"I promise!" Ashley slipped the necklace into his pocket.

They continued to walk and made their way towards the exit of LAX. As they did, they went past Tony who was at a fast food court eating a cheeseburger. Tony's alone, and besides the hamburger he also munched on fries and some fried rice. While he's digging in, he noticed a doting father play with his toddler son. Tony's transfixed and had a look of sadness upon his face. A look like he'd suffered a thousand personal tragedies in just one lifetime. He returned to his food and pushed the tray away. Tony's mobile vibrated.

"Wait." He took a serviette from the tray and a Bic pen from his pocket. "Yeah?" He started scribbling on the serviette. "Gazpacho." Tony hung up, and folded the serviette before placing it into the inner pocket of his jacket.

10

Los Angeles Airport, Part 2

An overweight 42 year-old guy in Bermuda shorts with greasy, shoulder length hair, stuffed fries in his mouth while occasionally sipping on a supersize Coke. He wore a T-shirt that read, 'I'm Chuck', which was indeed his name. He resembled a sleazier version of the Dude from the movie *The Big Lebowski*. As Chuck stuffed away, he flicked through a girly magazine before shooting an admiring look towards Jennifer, who was wearing a tight T-shirt that revealed she was quite well endowed. Jennifer walked hand-in-hand with Ashley, who carried a small rucksack on his back.

Ashley and Jennifer reached the entrance to an immigration checkpoint. Ashley put two comforting hands on Jennifer's shoulders. "Don't sweat it, Jen. I'll be back quicker than Arnie can say it. Have a blast in LA."

She hugged him tighter than a bear could. "Don't meet any New York City girls."

"Jen, don't believe everything that happens on TV."

"They'll eat you alive, Ash."

"I gotta move. Enjoy the sun. Catch a tan."

She slowly released her grip and he eased away while blowing kisses.

Jennifer waved goodbye, tears in her eyes. She started heading away, head bowed when Chuck bumped into her with his supersize coke, spilling some of it onto Jennifer's T-shirt.

"My T-shirt!"

"Heck, I'm sorry. I'm so clumsy!" Chuck tried

to dab her with a serviette.

"Stop, I got it."

"Shit, I'm a real klutz."

"No, I probably wasn't looking where I was going."

"Listen, let me pay for your dry cleaning or something." Chuck took his wallet and forked out 20 bucks.

"It's alright. I only got it at Joe-Mart. Didn't even cost 10 bucks."

"So buy yourself a new one, at a better mart. Go on take it."

Jennifer pocketed the cash.

"I still feel bad. Hey, can I get you a drink or something?" Chuck asked. His eyes were already probing her T-shirt. He wanted to salivate like Homer Simpson.

"No, I should be going. My boo gets real jealous."

"I ain't surprised. Beautiful girl like you. What you doing here anyway?"

"Erm... like my boyfriend's flying to New York."

"And he left you all alone? That ain't right. I can't imagine any dude having the strength to pull themselves away from a pretty little thing like you."

Jennifer frowned.

"On a downer, huh? So let me shout you a drink, lift you up, alright? Come on." Chuck ushered her away.

At a Starbucks, Jennifer sucked down a strawberry frappe. Chuck was getting aroused every time he heard her suck some of it.

"I was talking about a real drink."

"I'm only 18, remember?"

He didn't forget. "I gotta come clean, Jennifer. I didn't just accidentally bump into you. Before you freak, hear me out, alright? I'm actually casting for a new movie and I think you're the one."

Jennifer's eyes lit up like fairy lights on a Christmas tree. "A movie?"

"Yeah, we're auditioning tomorrow. You interested?"

"I don't know. I'm no actress."

"Not important. You learn on the go. Hell, if you can walk and talk at the same time, you can act."

"My boyfriend's an actor."

"Great. Hey, maybe he could be in it when he gets back?"

"I don't know, he's auditioning for a pretty big role. He'll be like super busy when he gets it."

"For sure. Hey, can you picture it, the two of you both starring in your own movies? How awesome would that be?"

"I guess."

"Take my business card and check out my website then you'll know it's all legit."

"I don't know if I should."

"It's just an audition, there's no obligation. Did you know that we pay $100 just for turning up?"

"A hundred bucks? For real?"

"And there'll be hamburgers and sodas too. So, what do you say? You'll come?"

Jennifer examined the business card. Snazzy lettering. "Why me?"

"Have you ever looked in a mirror? You're a babe! Movie star looks and none of that Hollywood, plastic fantastic, airbrushed crap. You're the real deal.

Genuine, beautiful – a girl other girls can relate to."

"You always, like, look for actors here and stuff?"

"No, I was dropping off a bud of mine. Discovering a peach of a girl like you, man, I'd normally have more chance being named MVP in the NBA."

Jennifer glanced at the business card again. "Alright Chuck, I'll do it. But, I don't think I'd feel, like, rightly comfortable going to your place alone."

"No problem. Tell ya what we'll meet here. How's noon tomorrow sound?"

11

Sheraton J.F.K. Airport Hotel, New York City

In a palatial hotel suite with an extensive bar and wall-to-wall copies of 'pretty' impressionist paintings, Ashley was perched on a luxurious sofa, flicking through the channels on a huge flat screen TV. He settled on an entertainment channel. Maybe one day he'd be featured.

He got up and wandered around the suite, picking up a French ceramic cup from the marble mantelpiece.

On the TV a news presenter reported, "In other entertainment news, murdered Bollywood star Ricki Singh was cremated today in Mumbai..."

Nicholas picked up the remote control and switched off the TV. "Do you like 19th century French ceramics?"

Startled, Ashley fumbled and almost dropped the ceramic cup. Nicholas strolled in holding a folded newspaper.

"Sorry. Mr Briddick. Hi."

Nicholas tossed the newspaper onto the coffee table. "Would you like a drink? Might help with the nerves." Nicholas warmly smiled then went to the bar and made himself a whiskey on the rocks.

Ashley kept his hands in his pockets, standing awkwardly. What should he do next?

"What do you want?" Nicholas asked.

"The part in your movie?"

Nicholas laughed a huge belly laugh. "I meant

for a drink."

"Oh, whatever."

Nicholas prepared a second whiskey on the rocks and handed it to Ashley.

Nicholas sat cross-legged on the sofa. "Take a seat."

"Thank you, sir."

Ashley perched himself on the edge of a gold-coloured armchair as Nicholas analysed him.

"Please, call me Nick. I hate formality."

"Alright, Nick. Never seen a hotel like this before. It's awesome."

"It'll do. It's only for a night before I fly back to London."

"What's it like in London?"

"It's just another big city you know, like New York."

"I ain't even seen New York yet. Just the airport."

"You've got time before you fly back to LA. You should check it out."

"I always wanted to see Times Square."

"I wouldn't bother if I were you, it's a nightmare. Crammed with tourists, gimmicks and fast food restaurants. Anyway, let's jump to it. You want to be in my film."

"Yeah, totally. I think I'd be great if you gave me the chance."

"What made you become an actor?" Nicholas swirled some of the whiskey around the inside of his mouth.

"When I was a kid I was always acting out. I swear, my dad used to give me a hiding sometimes cause I was like so loud. Whenever I got a chance to show off or do impersonations, man, I was doing it. I was born to be an actor, you know?"

"What kind of impersonations?"

"Oh man. Alright, I used to do Cartman, Jack Sparrow and Foghorn Leghorn."

"You can do Foghorn? I love that character. Do it now." Nicholas knocked back the rest of his whiskey.

Ashley swallowed some of his whiskey then cleared his throat. "I say, I say now. I'd really love a part in your new movie."

"Splendid. Well, if I ever make a live action film of Foghorn Leghorn, I'll give you a call. Another whiskey?"

"I'm still drinking this one."

"Come on, get your skates on then. I thought you Americans could handle your booze."

*

Back in L.A. at a cheap motel not far from LAX, a motel that could've doubled for the Bates Motel, Chuck had a digital camcorder fixed on a tripod, and had it set-up facing a double bed in a room that was the equivalent of porridge without honey or sugar. The honey was coming.

By the side of the bed was an open cardboard box with a Stetson Hat on top. A laptop was positioned on a corner table. Chuck, in a black T-shirt and again in those tasteless Bermuda shorts, continued setting everything up. Jennifer was on the edge of the bed, and on the edge generally, wearing short shorts and a T-shirt emblazoned with the name of a boy band, *Boyz Alive'*.

Jennifer fidgeted with her hair not knowing what to do. "You sure we gotta do this in a motel room?"

"Got no option till they finish fumigating the studio. Before we start, can I get you something?"

"No, I'm good."

"You sure? Don't want a soda? I've got loads."

"Alright."

Chuck covertly took a bottle of vodka and a bottle of coke out from the fridge. He grabbed a plastic cup and sneakily poured a shot of vodka into the Coke. Jennifer sat on her hands to stop herself from trembling. Chuck handed her the Coke.

Chuck got his own drink and raised it to toast. "Well, cheers!"

*

Meanwhile back at the Sheraton J.F.K. airport hotel, Ashley downed his third whiskey. He handed his glass over to Nicholas, who willingly poured him a new one.

"I've been through Wyoming on my way to Canada. Some beautiful country there. Have you been to Idaho?"

"Me and my cousin did a road trip this one time and went camping there. We got as far as Boise and had an awesome time. There was one night and, shit, we got so wasted."

"I love Idaho, there's something very unique, special and private about it. My film's about a bunch of teens, like you, with plenty of ambition but no outlet."

"Sounds like my life story."

"So with all the time, energy and testosterone of an average youth, they wreak havoc in their little hometown to try and wake it up out of its slumber."

"I could definitely be a part of this movie, Mr Briddick." Ashley burped.

"Nick, please. I'm looking for quite a few characters, including leads. However, it's important that we get the look exactly right."

"Believe me, I have that look and if I don't, heck, I'll change."

"Stand up. I want you to walk to the other side of the room. But add a slight swagger be a bit cocky."

Ashley did as he was instructed and demonstrated his best swagger, moving his hips from side to side and his shoulders going back and forth. "Like this?"

"I'm not sure. Maybe it's the outfit."

"What's wrong with it? It's what I always wear."

"Tell you what. Go into my room. You'll find some clothes spread out on the bed. They're the kind of style I imagine my character wearing."

*

In the cheap motel where chicken wings were 99 cents and ice was free, Chuck and a tipsy Jennifer laughed hysterically. They lay side-by-side, face-to-face, on the bed. An empty bottle of Coke was on its side on a coffee table.

"Whoa, what time is it?"

Jennifer hiccupped. "Time for you to get a watch!" She giggled.

"Have a watch, babe." Chuck winked then glanced at his watch. "Man, we have got to get this show on the road." He got behind the camcorder and checked the quality. "All's good. How about you, sweetness? You feeling good?"

She tried to sit up. "I think I'm drunk."

"No, you can't be. I mean, you can't get trashed from having a soda, right?"

He grabbed the Stetson cowboy hat and put it on Jennifer's head. "Now you're a real cowgirl."

"But I have no horse." Jennifer playfully pouted.

"Well, I think I know what we can do about that." Chuck returned to the camcorder and started recording. He picked up a clapperboard from inside the box and placed it in front of the camera. The clapperboard read, *'Chuck Loves to Fuck: Cowgirls'.*

"*'Chuck Loves to Fuck: Cowgirls'.* Action."

"What'd you say?"

"Nothing." Chuck put the clapperboard back into a box for next time. "Where you from, Jennifer?"

"Have you forgotten already? You know where I'm from."

"Alright, that's true. I did already ask. So, can you tell me how old you are?"

Jennifer hiccupped again. "I'm eighteen."

"Can you prove that?"

"Can I prove that? You wanna see my ID?"

"No, I believe you. So, you want to be in the movies, right? Who's your favourite actress?"

"Me!"

"And who's your favourite director?"

"You!"

"I like that answer."

Chuck played some up-tempo country music on his laptop. Jennifer reacted to it by attempting to dance sexily.

"You're so goddamn sexy. Why don't you take off your T-shirt?"

"I don't know."

"Just a little."

Jennifer bit her bottom lip, which made Chuck even more turned on than he already was and at that moment he was more turned on than Timothy Leary had ever been. She slid up part of her T-shirt revealing her torso and a bit of her bra. Her bra was virgin white.

*

Back in New York, Ashley re-emerged wearing some tight fitting jeans and an even tighter T-shirt that forced his muscles to bulge than they ever could naturally.

"They're very tight. I could barely get them on," Ashley said.

"We didn't have your exact measurements, now did we?"

"Yeah, right."

"All right, do that walk now. Don't forget make it cocky."

Ashley remembered all the movies he had seen with cocky individuals in them, and then those sports stars that came across as cocky. He put them all together and started walking like the cockiest person alive. His skin couldn't breathe, the clothes were that tight.

"Yes, that's it. Pretty good. Now in one scene there's a fight, so I want you to come towards me but in a really threatening way."

Ashley narrowed his eyes in a menacing fashion just like Robert De Niro had done in *'Heat'*, and *'Taxi Driver'* and every other film. Ashley threw up his clenched fists as he went towards Nicholas.

"Is that any good?"

"Yes but really angry, passionate. Like a hot-headed Italian."

Ashley went ultra De Niro with some Christian Bale thrown in.

"Good. Don't forget the swagger."

Ashley swaggered as he tensed his body, clenched his teeth, huffed and puffed like a ravenous tiger and put his fists up like a Mike Tyson in his prime. "You want me to say some dialogue or something?"

"Not at this moment. Right now it's all about the look."

"What do you reckon? You think I have the look?"

"Possibly. Let me see you with your shirt off."

"Say what?"

"Your shirt off. I need to see if you have a good body. I don't want one of my main characters to have a belly a dart's player would be proud of."

Ashley laboriously removed his T-shirt, revealing his lean yet muscular body.

"Mm, very Marky Mark. Try to make it look sensual. There's a scene with your character and a girl. I need to see whether you can pull it off."

Ashley put his T-shirt back on and stripped again like he was auditioning to become one of the Chippendales. "How's this?"

"Don't talk. Strip like you're making love."

Slowly and sensually, Ashley unbuttoned his jeans like he was still trying to persuade the woman he hoped to sleep with that she really should go through with it.

"Not bad, Ashley. You have the body. Come, take a seat and finish your whiskey. Maybe you'd like some champagne?"

"Cool. I love that shit." Ashley devoured the remainder of his whiskey.

Nicholas got a bottle of champagne from the fridge then started to uncork it. "You'll like this. It's Michel Dubois."

"Sounds French."

"It is French, like all champagne."

"At the wedding of my sis they had some champagne but it was from Oregon or something."

Nicholas popped open the champagne and poured two glasses. "Here, try this. It's lush."

Ashley tasted some and sloshed it around the inside of his mouth before taking a big, satisfactory swallow.

"Like a connoisseur, you are."

Ashley knocked back the whole glass and burped straight from the gut. "Hey, that fucking rocks."

Nicholas nestled himself comfortably next to Ashley. "You know, I think we need to do something with your hair." Nicholas caressed Ashley's hair similar to how a gay hairstylist would with a crush on his male client.

"What's up with my hair?"

"Nothing's really *wrong* with it, it's just that it's not really him."

"Who's him?"

"Jay, the character you might play. You see, Jay's a real rebel who falls in love with his enemy's sister."

"I like the sound of that. Being like an outlaw and getting the girl. Fuck yeah."

"Yes, it's a very pivotal moment. Almost Romeo and Juliet in its conception. They have a huge, passionate love scene."

"I'm down with that. I can do love scenes. I mean, I'm a great lover. Who's the actress?"

"We haven't cast her yet. Tell me Ashley, how are you downstairs?"

"What do you mean?"

"I mean, are you hung like a bull or hung like Mickey Mouse?"

"I'm doing pretty damn well. Are they going to see that?"

"They certainly will."

Ashley's mouth dropped open about five miles down. "Whoa. I've never done nude scenes before."

"Can you remove your jeans for me?"

"Err… Why?"

"I need to know. Do you want this part or not?"

"Damn right I do."

"Strip then."

Ashley unwillingly took off his jeans, taking them down super slow hoping that room service or something would interrupt them. His jeans were down, and were a struggle to pull off. It was like they were stuck on his legs with glue. "So?"

"And the boxers! When you make love to your girlfriend, do you make love with your boxers on or off?"

"Depends if we're in a rush or not."

"Well, we're not, so please remove them."

Ashley relented and took off his Calvin Klein's.

"Not bad, Ashley. Not bad." Nicholas zoomed in for a closer inspection and touched Ashley's penis. Ashley almost jumped out of his skin and took a step back, nearly falling over.

"What the fuck you doing?" Ashley was enraged.

"Just checking to see how photogenic it is. Sometimes body parts don't photograph well at all. I tell you what, we'll go to the bedroom."

"No fucking way." Ashley rapidly pulled up his boxers and the ever so tight jeans – which took a bit longer to pull up. He had to get back his other jeans.

"Sorry?" Nicholas queried.

"I think it's gone too far, you know?" Ashley was exposed, and alone.

Nicholas got up and moved over to the bedroom doors. He swiftly flung the doors open. "Let me give this to you straight, Ashley. I want to fuck you and I want you to fuck me. Now, either you get your arse into this bedroom or you go back to your little backwater town with your dreams in tatters."

"But, look, Mr Briddick. I'm not gay."

"I don't care if you're a monk, a gigolo or a raging homo. Do you want the part in this movie or lose your chance at Hollywood?"

"For sure I want the part but not like this."

"How do you think most actors make it? Haven't you ever heard of the casting couch?"

"Yeah, but I thought it only happened to hot chicks."

"You've got two choices. You can either leave this hotel and never, and I mean never, work in this industry again."

"What's the other?"

"You can come into this room and let me fuck your brains out and I promise you - no, I guarantee you - you'll be the big star you've always dreamt of becoming. What's it to be, Ashley?"

Ashley turned from one door to the other. His jacket was on a chair by a desk. He went over to it and paused.

"Bye, bye career," Nicholas said callously.

Ashley took out the necklace Jennifer had given him from his jacket pocket. He squeezed it tight then gave it a kiss, before facing Nicholas. He let the necklace slip from his fingers onto the cream-carpeted floor and gradually went into the bedroom. Nicholas slammed the door behind them.

*

The camcorder was still rolling in the LAX motel where the music had changed from up-tempo country to a heavier, dirtier, seedier hybrid of country and electronica – much like the grinding music from Peaches' song, *Fuck the Pain Away'*.

Jennifer, wearing the Stetson, was nude on all fours on the bed as Chuck pounded her from behind. His hairy belly was protruding and had to be lifted so he could do anything. Chuck spanked her bottom like he was whipping a horse, and in a moment that was reminiscent of the scene when Slim Pickens' character Major 'King' Kong rode the bomb in Dr Strangelove, he raised a hand in the air and shouted,

"Yee-haw!"

*

Meanwhile at the Sheraton J.F.K. hotel in New York City, Nicholas' hotel suite door was gently eased open. In crept Tony, in his black leather coat. Without a sound, he closed the door then sneaked over to the bedroom where sexual groans and painful moans were emanating.

Tony put one hand into his inner jacket pocket then ever so gently and quietly, opened the bedroom door and slipped inside. The bedroom was just as opulent as the rest of the suite, with a king-sized bed, French dresser and everything you'd expect for the king's ransom you'd pay per night.

On all fours, naked as the day he was born, was Ashley with a naked Nicholas roughly pounding him from behind. Ashley groaned in discomfort.

"Slowly!" Ashley pleaded.

Nicholas slapped Ashley's arse. "Shut up, bitch."

Tony moved like a ninja, closer to the bed and removed the latest iPhone from his pocket and had it ready to snap photos. In quick succession and with the skill and expertise of a teenage girl who spent way too long on her iPhone, Tony rapidly took photos. Nicholas and Ashley were startled and collapsed to the bed, Nicholas removing himself.

"Who the fuck are you?" Nicholas screamed.

"What's going on?" Ashley grabbed a pillow and covered his crotch.

Tony laughed heartily as he continued to take pictures. "Your wife say hello, Mr Briddick."

With the speed of a burglar that had one minute before the police arrived, Ashley gathered up his stuff and escaped out of the bedroom. Nicholas fell back onto the bed, hands covering his face.

*

The next day Ashley arrived back at LAX.

Defeat was in his eyes. His energy, enthusiasm and ambition had been forcibly removed as if someone had ripped out his still beating heart. He was a shadow of the man who had left LAX. His eyes had shadows and his hair had lost its sheen. As he walked, he winced in pain, though he tried to hide it when he spotted Jennifer standing at the exit to arrivals.

Jennifer had the same look as Ashley. Her loose, baggy jumper was worn to try to hide how uncomfortable she was and how disgusting she felt. She had picked up some sunglasses too and used them to further hide from everybody, as well as herself when she'd see herself in Ashley's eyes. She waved at him with as much enthusiasm as somebody waving from a prison cell.

They stood, frozen, a foot apart. Ashley attempted a smile, failed, and went back to straight face. "Hey Jen."

"Hey." Jennifer broke down into tears. She couldn't restrain herself any longer.

Ashley brought her into his arms and hugged her tighter than he ever had before. He was safe with her, and she was safe with him. Between them at that exact moment, nothing could divide them.

"I gotta tell... Ash, there's something..."

"Let's just go home."

Jennifer wiped away her tears with the sleeves of her jumper. "But what about... everything? Hollywood?"

"Fuck Hollywood." Ashley took the necklace from his pocket and placed it around Jennifer's neck. Then, hand in hand, they walked away gingerly like they had two steel rods stuck up their arses.

12

Heathrow Airport, London

Franz sat in a secluded section of a first class departure lounge. Leather sofas and arm chairs, menus to cater to all tastes and dietary requirements, and waiters that are on hand to fulfil any need. With each passing day, more distant from his late wife and from his former self, he was getting to become more of the psychiatrist – objective and cold.

Next to him on one of these fine leather sofas was a skinny, shy-looking Taiwanese boy. The Taiwanese boy stared at his feet.

Tony arrived, carrying that expensive-looking briefcase he'd gotten from the Japanese businessman. Franz stood up, holding the boy's hand. As they came together, Tony's face lit up like he was witnessing holding his child for the first time. The boy remained impassive.

"Marco!" Tony was elated and relieved at seeing the boy. The boy was unresponsive.

"Give me the briefcase," Franz said sternly.

Tony handed it over to Franz who sat back down with Marco. He then peered inside the briefcase.

"Good." Franz turned to Marco. "Go to your father."

Tony picked up Marco in a tight hug, cuddling and kissing him repeatedly as though he hadn't seen him in years. "It's over now. You're okay." Tony looked at Franz straight in the eyes. "Contract finished? It's over?"

"You have your son." Franz hurried away with the briefcase.

Tony took out his mobile, not letting go of his son. A smile continued to beam across Tony's face like the first sunlight of the day. He spoke into his mobile, "Yes. We're coming home."

The End

www.ingramcontent.com/pod-product-compliance
Lightning Source LLC
Chambersburg PA
CBHW032050180726
48284CB00004B/1272